Torn between me and you.

In loving memory of Eric (Ej) Smith Sr.
Acknowledgements I would like to thank Billy Walker for typing and being supportive every step of the way, Suhkarri Dailey for the illustration, Amber Henderson for editing the book and being an awesome best friend throughout the past 10 years. Special thanks to my mother, India Bunch, who too wrote a book and encouraged me not only with writing a book but with life itself. Lastly, I would like to thank my friends and family who believed I could achieve this goal.

Prologue

"State of Illinois vs Elijah Davis Jr. In the case #P0298751, how do you plead?"

"Guilty!" Elijah answered the judge with his head held high.

"Mr. Davis before I sentence you, do you have anything to say?" the judge asked.

With a calm voice, Elijah said, "What should I say, I apologize? No. I know what I did. Just give me my time. I do wanna apologize to my mom, though." He turned to look at her, "You lost Dad to the streets, and now I'm lost to the system." He turned back.

"Well, now that that's over," the judge started, "back to what we're here for. In the murder of..."

"My baby!" A woman that appeared to be Elijah's mother yelled.

Elijah turned around with a tear falling down his face, spoke in a soft voice, "I'm sorry Ma, I ain't mean to hurt you. I was always taught what goes around comes around. And even if you didn't do what was done to you, you did something."

What The Gutter Took From Me
Chapter 1

For as long as I can remember, I woke up every October 20th at 6:25am. It never failed. As many times as I was told the story, shit, I still break out in sweats every time. I have dreams about it, as if I was there. Auntie called Mama and it kind of makes sense now. Around that same time, five minutes before, she called. It's like I couldn't stay asleep. I kept moving, hell, I jumped so hard I cried. Mama jumped. She thought it was the dog.

I had never seen Mama cry until that day. Auntie called Mama and said she heard shots while getting ready for work. Auntie's neighbor came knocking and told her my dad was lying in the street, lifeless. Mama told me she ran almost 20 city blocks, even though she had a car. When my mama got there, she started trippin' trying to call my dad's phone. It was like she knew he was dead. They had already moved him. So I didn't get why she was calling, and even called from different phones. Ever since, each year I wake up at that time, sweating. I heard stories from everybody about the kind of man my dad was. He was nothing nice. A savage with a good heart, who did stuff sometimes. I hear I act just like him.

My name is Elijah, but everybody calls me Lil' Eli. I lost my pops a week after my first birthday. I know y'all tryna figure out how I remember the way things went when Pops died. Hell, I don't even know. I'm still trying to figure out why I sweat so damn hard on his death day.

I just started at this new school in the 'burbs. They lame out here, cornball ass niggas. I'm supposed to be getting ready for school but Imma just wait until my mama yells up here. I don't understand why I couldn't just keep going to school by my granny crib. My mama talking about "a better life". So, that means she had to work 10 times harder for this "better life". We were never poor. She always had a good job. We were cool, if you ask me. She wanted to get far away from the hood. I mean a few of my homeboys got locked up and even some made it to see my daddy up above. Nah, let me stop lying. Them niggas probably kicking it in hell, all the shit we did, but what that gotta do with me? I'm only like 30 minutes from my granny crib so I'ont really trip. The crib out here is cool. It's really quiet. I don't have to watch over my shoulder how I do in the hood. These lil' suburban hoes got a lil class to them, and money, too. I need to get me a "Bev" to check her crib out, me and my boy, Derek. I know we can get some nice shit. I need to get Mama a gift. I try to make up for my dad, even though the heffa got a lil' boyfriend. I still get mad at her for that, but I guess she gotta live, too. This nigga bonded me out and was at every court date, so I guess he cool. But if his sweet ass thinks I'm calling him anything other than his name, he got another thing coming. Which reminds me, I got court for that case he bonded me out for. It was a hit and run, and I made a mistake and ran the nigga over. I was into it with the nigga. This hoe ass man told the police it was on purpose. Even if it was, fuck you telling for? You in the streets. Just take that shit like a man, and if you feel froggy then jump, my nigga. I'll be glad when that shit over, though. My mama paid a good lawyer. This my last year of high school. Then, I told her I'll go away to college. She worries about me too much. I'm only going to make her happy. If it was up to me, I'll be chilling, making money. I'm no dummy. I just be having other stuff to do with my time like robbing, shooting dice, kicking it with my people, going to parties, and getting up with my lil' female. See, my mama don't understand that, talking bout "that's what the weekend is for, to kick it". She don't know about the robbing, and I prefer to keep it that way.

My mom yelled from downstairs, "Elijah, get up! I'm not understanding why I still have to be your DAMN alarm clock. What you got a phone for?"

I yelled back down to her, "I'm not understanding why you don't wanna be!" I laughed when he heard footsteps coming. She opened the door and I was sitting on my bed laughing.

"I'm funny?" she asked me.

"I wouldn't say funny, but I just don't see why you can't wake me up, lay my clothes out, and have my food fixed," I smirked.

"Boy, it's cereal down there, and you might not have time to eat that," she shot back.

"Cereal??" I asked with a funny look on my face. "So basically, I'm not good enough for a home cooked meal."

"If you get up early enough", she stated.

"Don't expect nothing on Mother's Day, not even a bowl of cereal", I laughed. "Karma, karma"

She laughed and hit me in a playful way. "Come on boy, we gotta go."

"Hold on Ma," I stopped. "Why I gotta leave with you?"

"Because I'm your mama and I said so," she looked at him.

I smiled, "So, I can't say or tell you nun' huh?

Walking out of my room, she replied, 'Damn right!"

New School, Same Mentality
Chapter 2

First day at this wack ass school, and I'm lost. I don't wanna ask nobody shit 'cause they might think we cool. I'll find the office myself! Should've played sick or some'. My mama wasn't going for that, though.

"Excuse me, young man, you need help with something today? Are you lost?" Asked a man, who looked important like he could be the Dean or even the Principal.

"Do I look lost?" I snapped.

"Yeah, you must be new here, getting smart with me like that," the man stated firmly, taken aback by my blunt attitude.

"My bad. I didn't know I was getting smart, but yeah I'm looking for the office. Pretty sure you can get me there, right?" I laughed.

"Aye, I like you, kid. Follow me", the man chuckled, "What's ya name?"

"Elijah Davis. Get me to the office a lil' quicker and you'll be able to check my records and get my age, grade, credits and whatever else you need."

The man smirked and said, "Mr. Davis, I'm gonna let you find the office yourself."

"Nah, my bad, stop playing," I laughed.

"It's right here. I'll take you to your first class," the man offered.

"Or I can miss it," I smiled.

"Or you can sit in morning and after school detention. Try me. I'm Dean Blade by the way."

We both laughed.

"You got two minutes, so let me get you there. Where you come from, boy?" Dean Blade asked.

"Can you expand on what ya mean? I don't want you to think I'm getting smart." I said sincerely.

"What school did you come from?" Dean Blade asked.

"Aw, from CLR High School out west," I stated.

The bell rings.

"Well, if you have any questions, you know where the office is," Dean Blade stated.

"Alright, good looking, by the way," I thanked him, walking into my first class.

"Well, Good morning, you must be Mr. Davis, our new student! I'm Ms. Gipson," spoke an older white lady, with the squeakiest voice ever.

"Yeah, I mean yes," I corrected myself.

"Well, take a seat. Anywhere is fine," she insisted.

Man, I'm walking to my seat, trying so hard not to laugh. These niggas look lame as hell. Big clothes, durag, fat ass Mikes on. I looked around and spotted an old female of mine by the name of Endia, and found a seat right next to her. Lil' pretty ass face, nice curly hair, looking like she mixed with some of everything. She still got a nice shape and slight stomach. Yeah, I'm trapping this hoe. I refuse for my baby to be bald-headed like my mama.

"Is this seat taken?" I asked her, with a sly smile.

"No, you can sit here," she answered. "Let me just move my bag."

I had already known Endia before this school. It was like we were reunited.

We both laughed out loud as I sat down next to her.

"Care to share the joke, Ms. Monroe?" Ms. Gipson asked.

"It wasn't a joke. I apologize for the outburst. I was helping the new student," Endia apologized.

"Okay class, start chapters 3-6. Whatever you don't finish becomes homework. Ms. Monroe, do you mind catching Mr. Davis up?" Ms. Gipson asked Endia.

"Yes please," I smiled at Endia.

"Sure," she smiled back.

"So Endia, where yo lil boyfriend at? I'ont wanna get you in trouble for getting me caught up in this class," I smirked.

"I don't have a boyfriend, but thanks for asking," she rolled her eyes, "and what about you and yo lil' dusty?"

"Talking 'bout dusty," I chuckled, "baby, I don't fuck with dusties. If that's the case, remember you was one? I must look like a dusty nigga to you or something."

"No, but," she started.

"Ain't no but," I stopped her, "I judge people off the people they mess with, if that makes sense? So, if you think I mess with a nothing ass wild female, then I'm a reflection of what I mess with. Remember you messed with me? Come on, give me more credit baby."

"Okay, whatever. I was just playing," she rolled her eyes.

"I'm tryna make you my dusty again," I smirked, nudging her arm playfully.

Endia laughed.

"Let's get back to work before Ms. Gipson comes asking questions," Endia urged. "Since you decided to come a few days late, you have to catch up to us. From 1-3, it'll be a mini quiz which she'll give you before we leave."

"You can just give me the answers, right?" I asked playfully.

"Um, no. Why would I do your work for you?" she asked quizzically, furrowing her eyebrows.

I smiled. As we started reading the chapters, my phone kept going off.

"Can you put yo phone on silent? That vibrating is irritating me," Endia said with a slight attitude.

"Girl, you must want my number. This not bothering you."

"Nope, I'll pass. I just wanna finish this so I won't have to later," she stated smartly.

I stared at her, smirked, then finished reading the book.

My phone vibrated again. I ignored it. It vibrated again.

"You gone get that?" Endia asked with attitude.

"You gone mind yo business?" I shot back.

Endia started to say something but stopped herself. At that time, the bell rang.

"Don't sit next to me anymore. Thanks," she stated, gathering her things.

"Girl, who? I'm sitting next to you every time," I stated back.

We both laughed.

"So, what's yo next class?" I asked.

"You gone take me to it?" she asked back, smirking.

"Can you just answer the question, psycho?" I laughed.

"Oh, it's up the stairs, make a left, then end of the hall," she told me.

"Aite, good looking. You can still put yo number in here," I insisted.

"I'll still pass." She walked off, smiling.

As I walked down the hall, I started thinking to myself about how I would get her again, but my thoughts were interrupted.

"Wassup, Bro?" a tall light skinned boy greeted me.

"Wassup?" I looked at him skeptically as he approached me.

"Damn, you don't remember me, bro?" he asked me.

"Nah, you know me or some?" I asked back, furrowing my eyebrows.

"You be with Derek, right?" he tilted his head to the side.

"I'ont know who Derek is. I'm late for class," I stated, walking off.

"Damn, bro, you just gon' diss me like that?" he asked, holding his arms out.

"What's yo name, anyway?" I asked, turning back to him.

"Curt," he stated.

"Aite," I nodded, walking off, leaving Curt standing alone.

As the day went by, I dragged to each class. I was out of the building by the time the bell could even finish ringing.

"Aye Ma, can you run me to Granny crib?" I asked her, as I walked in the crib.

"No, I'm not doing shit on my off day," she stated.

"Aite, remember that," I nodded my head, pointing at her.

"And don't call none of yo thug, dirty, gang banging ass friends to my house. They better meet you on the eway," she rolled her eyes.

"Eway? Let me see yo car," I smiled.

"Aha! You still owe me $2,500 from getting my shit impounded," she shut me down.

I shook my head and walked towards my room, pulling my phone out to make a call.

"Where you at, Derek?" I asked my righthand man.

"Leaving this girl crib," he answered.

"I got some for us. Come and grab me," I told him.

"Yo mama there?" he asked.

"Yeah, why?" I asked back, quizzically.

"Man, hell naw! Yo ass better walk to the corner. You know Rose always talking," Derek stated quickly.

"Boy, what the fuck you scared of?" I asked.

"Yo mama."

"My mama!?" I laughed out loud.

"Nah, she be tweakin'. I'll be there in like 20 minutes. Yo ass better be on the corner."

Call ended.

It feels like I'm forgetting something. I got everything, though. Anyway, Derek, that's my main man. We've been through everything together from getting shot at, getting locked up, graduating, fighting, hoes, you name it. We always split everything. His only big brother was killed, and that's who taught us everything we know. His mama is an alcoholic and his daddy was never around. So, all he got now is his grandma, our lil' homie Coby, and me. That's how I look at it. His brother grew up right under my old man. From the stories we heard, he was getting close to finding out who killed my pops, but he ended up getting whacked. He looked up to my pops and took his death hard. Anything I needed, he was on it. Anything I wanted, I got it. I pray to God every night two times that I find the nigga that did that to them and I make it home to my mama.

My phone started ringing. It was Derek.

"Come out," he said.

"Alright, here I come," I replied.

"Man, yo scary ass ain't never park three houses down," I joked as I walked to the car.

We both laughed.

"You made some friends at that wack ass school?" Derek teased.

"Shid, I'm not trying to," I shrugged.

"You need to. They ass got some' we don't," Derek frowned.

"What's that?" I asked.

"Money!!" he yelled.

"What you mean? We can get they sweet ass," I stated.

"You need to be making friends," he told me.

"Be patient, bro. Let this shit play out. You be too thirsty," I shook my head.

"I want that money," Derek stated, not trying to hear what I was saying.

"We gon' get it! Anyway, this lil' thirsty ass nigga brought you up earlier." I told him.

"Who?" he asked, surprisingly.

"Some lame ass nigga. He knew I be with you. He came up saying my name, then asked don't I be with you. I was tryna study this nigga face, tryna see where we know him from," I said, thinking back to earlier.

"What's the name?" Derek asked.

"Curt. He tall, light skinned with freckles, got some fat ass eyebrows, with that dumb ass sponge hair that everybody wear. You can tell he a lame ass nigga," I laughed.

"How the fuck he know us?" Derek wanted to know.

"I'ont even know his ass. He was friendly. I wasn't with that shit. He looked familiar, though. Imma find out." I stated, nodding my head.

"Yeah, find out." Derek rubbed his chin.

"Slam just texted me. He said grab him." I told Derek.

"Tell him aite, but ay, you ain't been getting no funny vibe from him lately?" he asked me, skeptically.

"What you mean?" I looked at him.

"He just been thirsty. Maybe I'm tweaking," he shrugged.

"Yeah, shorty, you do be over thinking. He just wanna kick it. He always been thirsty," I waved him off.

Slam, that's our other homie. He moved in the hood like three years ago. That's Big Man's cousin from out of town. We all ended up getting cool when Big Man got locked up. I'ont know why Derek be tripping. He don't be wanting Slam hitting no licks with us or nothing. All he allow him to do is kick it, and barely that. Derek be paranoid, anyway. He feels like Slam not like us, so he always keeps it brief with him. Slam messed up a lick once before. It was a robbery gone bad. This nigga shot the girl we was robbing in the head, by accident. What made it so bad was it was Derek's lick. So, all we came back with was a dead body on our hands, a couple of twenties a piece, and a 10 pc nugget meal. This nigga was so mad Slam grabbed the food. Ever since then, Derek ain't been vibing with Slam. Slam be feeling the vibe, though. He still tries, but that nigga Derek stubborn.

"Shorty, this the house right here. They schedule never change. They got a lil' arm dog that ain't gone do shit. They take a family jog for at least 30 minutes, so that gives us time to be in and out. We ain't gotta break shit. I'm not sure if they got a security system, but they probably do. Sina, the white girl who crib it is, got a bag," I told him.

"Bumping his daughter?" Derek asked, jokingly.

"Nope, the maid who couldn't make it in today," I smirked.

"There they go," Derek pointed out, as we watched the family walk out the house.

Typical white family; husband, wife, son, and daughter.

"We going for everything once they hit the block," I said to Derek, watching them closely.

Man, these dumb ass people basically invited us in. The door was cracked open. Guess they must have thought they closed it. I don't give a fuck! We grabbed everything. Jewelry, two TV's, a laptop, a brand new Louie belt, and shoes. We even found a stack in his drawer. We was in and out. We was even nice enough to close and lock the door for them. We wasn't tryna be greedy 'cause that's how you get put in jams. We dropped everything off at Derek's grandmother's crib. We had one more hit to do before we grabbed Slam. Derek had one for us. This nigga wanted to rob the dice game. Shid, we had our gun on us, so we was ready for whatever. We know these niggas, but they ain't our niggas so its whatever. We parked right around the corner. We snuck through the gangway. Them niggas didn't even know we stood there for a few seconds.

"Man, get y'all bitch ass up! We need everything!" Derek said to the boys on the ground.

One of them slowly tried to reach for his piece and Derek and I both blew his ass down. This robbery didn't go wrong. The nigga had it coming. You see two niggas with guns and you decide to up yours? Okay, cool. Gave his ass a taste of who not to play with. Dude we just smoked, dropped his piece and I picked it up right along with everything in his pockets. I even took the nigga gum. My breath was a lil' tart, anyway. After we got everything, we took off down the street not knowing as we made it back to the car, the police would be pulling up to write us a ticket. When they saw us with all black and masks, they said fuck the ticket and got on our ass. I instantly took the wheel. I was high speed ready, anyway. I left they ass in the dust. I was hitting alleys and sidewalks. They ass wasn't catching up.

We play back

Chapter 3

After we made it back to Derek's crib, we saw Slam sitting in the front. After me and Derek split everything we made today, we kicked it with Slam for a minute then I left. I caught a cab to the crib. The police was probably still looking for us. My mama ass wants me to get a job. I sell weed and rob. Her ass better be lucky I got time for school. When I made it home, her ass was gone. Shid, I was cool with that. I went straight in, cleaned up, got in the shower, did the lil' chapters, and went to sleep.

The next day I got up, knocked that school shit out, got Endia and two other female numbers, then I went straight to the hood. I was hoping I seen the nigga Curt to ask him how he knew us. In the middle of my thoughts, Slam called me to tell me some niggas just shot at him. First thing that came to my mind was dude nem from last night. We had masks on so, how? I get to Derek's crib and Slam already there.

"You recognized one of their faces?" Derek asked Slam.

"Yeah, dude who be with TB nem. The nigga wit the hair," Slam answered.

"You talking about Skunk?" Derek turned his face up.

"Yeah, his hoe ass. I was leaving out the store and we looked at each other. He pulled his piece out and instantly started blowing. He shot a lil' boy and some older lady," Slam explained.

"Damn! What he on you for?" Derek asked.

"Man, I don't know. It caught me off guard," Slam answered.

"What you do?" I asked him.

"Man, SHIT!" Slam said, loudly.

"What you getting loud for? My grandma in there," Derek said through clenched teeth.

"Aite, we can slide on them niggas. What you wanna do Derek?" I looked at him.

"I'm on whatever you on, Eli," Derek answered.

"Aite, we gone."

A few hours later, them niggas was back out like nothing happened. We all walked up letting bullets ride. We hit at least six of them niggas. The rest of them took off. At least we hit, though. That's all I cared about. I made sure the two I hit wasn't breathing. That was foul for them to shoot while that old lady and shorty was right there. Shid, they the ones who should get passes; old people, kids, and innocent women. I say innocent women because some of them be with the set up. So, some of these females deserve to die. Not to sound mean but stay in yo lane bitch, and be the queen that you were born to be. Niggas don't understand that, though. Anyway, once our job was done, we took off. After that, the streets was hot. Not a soul out walking the streets. Niggas was scared and that was cool 'cause kids was able to play. Derek got word that niggas wanted to squash the beef. Honestly, I was cool with it, but me and Derek was both curious on where the beef came from. I told Derek we can squash it, but we needed to know where the animosity came from. We was never buddy buddy with them, but we was cordial. No bad beef. So, it put me in deep thought like what did Slam leave out? 'Cause now that I think about it, that story don't make sense. Why would you and the nigga mug each other if ain't no beef? Better yet, why would a nigga start randomly blowing at you if it ain't beef? I had too much shit on my mind.

The next day at school, I ran into the nigga, Curt. Everything had me paranoid.

"Wassup, Elijah?" he greeted me.

"Aye bro, how you know me and D again?" I got straight to the point.

"Huh? What you mean? Who don't know you?" he chuckled.

"I'm asking how, though? I just got to this school. My first day here you knew me by name and I never seen you. So, wassup? Who you know? What's to you?" I questioned him.

I started getting mad 'cause the nigga wasn't answering my questions fast enough. Did he know somethin'? This what I didn't need. Me and Derek did a lot, so I'm tryna see where this nigga fit in at.

"I don't know y'all, but I heard of y'all. Well, y'all used to hustle with Big Man on Luther Drive until he got sent down state," Curt explained.

"How you know Big Man?" I asked, quizzically.

"That's Shaunni's baby daddy. Shaunni's my Sister," he answered.

"Bre's cousin Shaunni?"

"Yeah. I don't know you personally. I just remembered y'all was who he rode with when he was out, and y'all had his back," Curt replied.

"Mm-hm, aite." I nodded my head.

"So, we good, Elijah?" Curt asked.

"Call me Eli and make sure he gets my number," I stated, giving him my number.

I remembered the shorty. He used to always be under Big Man. Big Man looked out for Curt. Curt used to get punched on, and he was dirty back then. That nigga got big as hell. Big Man was like his brother. Before he got booked, we hit a nasty lick. He got caught for it and never said me or D names. That was love. They caught him with a gun, so that gave him hella Fed time. It was fucked up 'cause we robbed a federal agent.

We stopped seeing Shaunni, though. I heard they moved and she changed her number. We lost contact. We was giving her whatever she needed, including money for him. I forgot about her lil' brother tho. Big Man left Shaunni with money. She probably still sitting on some. We was getting big money at the time . We slowed down after that, though. I haven't seen her in almost two years.

"You talked to Big Man lately?" I asked Curt.

"Yeah, my sister does," he answered.

"Let me know if y'all need some. Give him my number." I told him again.

I saw Endia in the hall. I knew she was mad. I just didn't know why. When I walked up and got closer, I saw her standing with one of the girls whose number I got the same day I got hers. Endia was a playa', though. She ain't front my move or nothing. Tisha, who happened to be her friend, was extra. I knew I was gon' hit and keep going. I didn't know her and Endia knew each other, though. All I knew was I wanted Endia, so I was gon' make that clear right there. I was still gon' bump Tisha, though 'cause I know she going and don't care.

"Come here, Elijah," Tisha called to me.

"Wassup, homie? Wassup, Endia?" I smiled, innocently at Endia.

"Mm-hm," Endia rolled her eyes.

"So, you tried to talk to me and my friend?" Tisha asked me with an attitude.

"Nah. I was tryna talk to Endia. You asked for my number. I ain't know you was on that," I lied, with a straight face. I knew she was on that. Shid, I was, too.

"I guess," she rolled her eyes, "come on Endia. Niggas is nothing."

"Nah, she gon' stay right here for a min," I stated, matter-of-factly.

Tisha looked at Endia and by the look on Endia's face, Tisha knew Endia wasn't gon' budge.

"Aite, girl. I'll see you." Tisha walked away.

"Alright," Endia said to her.

"What's yo problem?" I asked her, smiling.

"You tryna make me lose your number 'cause you wanna be thirsty?"

"Man, she came at me," I explained.

"So, that means give yo number out or exchange?" she raised her voice.

"Nah, it don't," I answered her, softly.

"Right, act like it," she stated.

"So, that's why you haven't been replying to me?" I looked her in the eyes.

"Yep."

"So, when we gon' spend some time outside these walls?" I asked her, smirking.

"Whenever you're ready to take me out," she stated.

"Tonight?" I urged.

"That's fine. You can pick me up at 8."

"Alright," I smiled.

"And delete them numbers right now," she demanded.

"Okay," I chuckled.

"I said now!"

I laughed and did what she said to stay on her good side.

Later on that night, I picked Endia up. She already looked mixed, the outfit she had on ain't make it no better. She had on a nice cream dress that showed every curve she had.

After we left the restaurant, I told her I needed to run home for a second. The minute we pulled into the driveway, it wasn't hard to get her upstairs. Before she knew it, I was taking everything off of her. I'm glad it was a Friday 'cause I had to show out and show her what my mouth and piece was like. I wish she would've told me she was a virgin, though. I started kissing on her. She was steady laughing and moving over. I nipped that in the bud, went down on her and changed her life. When I tried to go in, it was way too tight. This mf was a virgin, but I was already in and it felt so good. I was willing to deal with the craziness that was gon' come behind this. I knew she was gon' think she was my girl afterwards. After we were done, I took her home. I peeped the whole block. They ass got money. I slid on the block with Derek and a few more of the guys told them about Big Man and Curt.

"I thought yall forgot about Big Man," Slam said.

"Why? 'Cause you came around? Nigga, you ain't on his level. That's a different breed of a nigga," Derek checked him.

"So, what you saying Derek?" Slam asked, shocked by Derek's outburst.

"How it sound? Fuck do it matter if we forgot about him or not?" Derek fumed. "You wanna be him or some'?"

"Nah, I don't give a fuck," Slam shrugged.

"Right! You Eli's homie. Anyway, I'm tryna see how the fuck we get caught in a jam and don't even know what happened?" Derek questioned.

"Nigga, I told you that fool started shooting for nothin'," Slam stated, loudly.

"Aite, y'all trippin'. It don't matter. We gon' get to the bottom of this shoot out shit. And as far as Big Man, why does it matter, Slam? What's to you?" I asked him, skeptically.

"Nothin'. I was playing, Niggas getting offended," Slam answered, looking at Derek.

"Y'all seen any of them niggas?" I asked them both, switching the subject.

"Nah," Slam answered first.

"TB was on his porch when my girl rode past. It was just him," Derek answered next.

"I'm 'bout to slide. I'll get up with y'all ina min," Slam cut the conversation short.

"Aite, be smooth, bro. Hit the phone," I told him.

"Man, shorty, I say let's go holla at TB if he's still out to see what's what," Derek stated.

"That nigga gone try and shoot, hell naw," I said, looking at him as if he was crazy.

"Get yo scary ass. We both got our piece. We good," Derek assured me.

"Aite, bet. This nigga get tough, we blowing his ass down," I stated.

"Man, don't start that hot shit. You gon' get us in a bigger jam than we already in. Just be cool, bro. Let me talk," he insisted, as we left to find TB.

We get to the nigga crib and he instantly reach for his piece. Shid, I had my piece ready. Derek tryna play peace keeper.

"Man, put y'all shit up! We came to talk. It's enough blood on both sides. I'm tryna get to the bottom of this," Derek stated, with his hands up.

As we both put our pieces up, Derek asked, "What happened with Slam? How did it start?"

"Man, that nigga Slam was doing too much. We letting this nigga eat and taking care of him. I'm tryna figure out how he tell on one of the guys and dropped the location for the opps to get up with us. Them niggas wasn't watching that hard," TB explained.

"What you mean, he told on one of the guys?"

"Man, they picked Rufus and Slam up. They did a robbery together, but Rufus not home and Slam is. He say the man was in there telling everything. Slam home while Rufus still there with no bond. They charged him with pills, a gun, and a home invasion. This rat ass nigga out chilling like ain't shit happened. Then, you know my girl, her cousin Zae from the other side, she overheard them talking about how Slam even running with them! Like damn nigga, how hungry are you?" TB fumed.

"Like what you really on? You from this side, yet you giving the police and the opps info on us. These niggas ain't know where we been hustling. Now every time we dip off, we having shootouts. So, when my brother saw Slam, he tossed at him. 'Cause, Derek nigga, when you lost his gun, we gave him one. And Eli nigga, when you fucked his money up from the weed, we helped him get back. So why fuck over us?" TB was going off.

"Lost a gun? What the fuck you mean, lost his gun? This nigga ain't own a gun! I let that nigga use my shit! If I ain't got shit, nigga, I got guns," Derek boasted.

I couldn't do shit but laugh 'cause this nigga was working for me and fucked my money up. I gave him a pass, though. Derek always said it was some to the nigga, but I thought he was just talking. He getting us into it. He getting TB nem into it. Fuck he getting outta this? He even talking to the police. Now that had me thinking 'cause I'ont like having to watch niggas around me.

"It's funny cause he said yo brother just started shooting for nothin'," I told TB.

"Man, I knew it was some extra shit going on. I knew it was some' weird about that nigga, right when I thought I was tripping," Derek snapped.

"What's the point, though?" TB questioned.

"We gon' be cool about it. He ain't gotta know we know shit. I wanna see where he's going with this," I rubbed my chin.

"Man, I'm ready to pop his bitch ass," Derek fumed.

After we finished talking to TB, everything was squashed. They was on Slam ass and we was out the way at this point. He not gon' ever know this convo happened. Everything will eventually come out, though. Derek was pissed. He wanted to pull up on Slam and blow his ass down. I'm usually the one ready to knock a nigga head off, but lately I've been chillin and thinking things out. How could this nigga not only lie on us but to us? That night we went to get his lick back, I hit three people and two didn't make it. Derek hit one and this nigga Slam ain't score at all. Now, I'm thinking this was all a part of his plan. But why? Why put us in a jam? If we confront the nigga, he gon' play dumb. I'ont know how to holla at him 'cause if he say the wrong thing or something the wrong way, I might beat his ass or leg him. It's just certain stuff you don't do to yo own people.

What's The Motive

Chapter 4

Imma holla at my mama. She's from the streets, so I know whatever she says, it's gon' be a hunnit. I'ont need her boyfriend shiny head ass putting his input in on this .This gon' have to be a one on one session. I think I hear them pulling up now.

"My dishes better be clean! The garbage better be taken out! And bet not no lil' heffa be in my house!" she yelled.

"Aye, Ma," I called down to her.

"Aye, Elijah," she mocked me.

"Come here, real quick. I'm tryna see some'." I told her.

"Yo ass prolly tryna beg, and stop yelling in my damn house! You better come down here," she told me.

"You started yelling first, talking about some dishes. You need to have more kids. You still be telling me to come here and pass you the remote like I'm a shorty or some'," I teased.

"Boy, who you talking to? Matter fact, let me come up there and make sure we on the same page," she said, as she walked up the stairs.

Now, my mama uses this same excuse every time, "when I was younger, my hair was long but I got a perm". Man, my mama got a curly fro. It hasn't grown since I knew her and that's been all my life. She got oily looking skin but without the oil, type brown skin. I use to get mad when niggas use to stare at her butt. I used to block it so they wouldn't look, but after a while I gave up. She's 5'5' with light hazel brown eyes.

"Now, what about you going to get a remote, after I took care of you and everything else up until now?" she teased.

"Ma, you be so extra. Anyway, I need to holla at you," I told her.

She cut me off. "If you got a baby on the way, I got the abortion money and you paying me back. I'm still taking care of you. Ain't no grown ass female moving in my house. When I had you, I was on my own. You still playing these street games. Uh-uh, get yourself together first, then maybe we can talk on the decision."

"Boyyy, what is you talking about? I haven't said nothin' about no kids," I laughed.

"Aw, well disregard that. Better yet, remember that 'cause I'm not gon' repeat myself. I'm not taking care of no baby unless you dead or in jail and I'ont have to worry about that. So, what you wanna talk about?" she asked.

"Man, you crazy. But anyway, the nigga Slam."

"The one you and Derek started kicking it with?" she asked, tilting her head.

"Yeah. He moved on Butterfield like two years ago. Anyway, we started kicking it with him. He was more of my homie than he was Derek's. Derek was always iffy about him but dealt with him just off the strength of me. But now, I'm iffy about him, too. So, the other night, you saw the news when the lil' boy and old lady got shot?" I asked her.

"He did it?" she raised her eyebrows.

"Nah, Ma. But a nigga was shooting at him and missed and hit them. But anyway, he tells us, so you know it's whatever with me and Derek. We go to they lil' spot. The niggas was sweet. They was out kicking it like ain't nothin' ever happened. Me and D knock three a piece down. This man, Slam, missed, but we wasn't tripping. Maybe he not a shooter, cool, but then Derek get word the niggas wanna squash it. Ma, you know I'm always ready just in case a nigga act crazy, on Pops."

She shook her head.

I finished. "We go to one of the niggas crib unannounced. He reached for his and I reached for mine. Derek stopped it before it got ugly. Long story short, we talked to the nigga and in so many words, Slam lied and said I messed his money up. Ma, you know this nigga was working for me and jagged some money. But, I gave him a pass. He also lied and said Derek lost his gun. Nigga, what you need a gun for if you always calling us? The nigga prolly don't even know what he doing with a gun. That was D's gun. So, he got these niggas thinking we just messing him over. So, they helped him out. Man, why the dude we went to see tell us Slam told the police on they homie. Then, he told the opps every location on them. You know how I feel about loyalty. I might bust that nigga in his mouth if I say some. So, how should I go about it? 'Cause D ready to do whatever 'cause nigga, if you in the streets, ain't no telling. You don't talk. If you can't handle that, stay in the crib." I shrugged.

"Well, first off, I asked God for a daughter. I should be hearing about how she bossed up on a nigga who he broke her heart, and me telling her something that a proud mother should say." She shook her head.

"But when I hurt a girl by mistake, I'm getting cursed out." I rolled my eyes, playfully.

"Because you don't care about them for real, but that's for another time, after this mess. Well first off, I never liked him cause like D said it was always something to him. You gotta be ahead of him at all times. You can't let this sneaky, snake ass nigga beat you at this game. You and Derek are a different breed. Y'all can't teach a nigga how to be real or how to be loyal. He set this up. He knew y'all would ride for him, and I told yo monkey ass about that, anyway. Stop jumping for niggas who wouldn't do the same for you, or even send you shit if you was locked up, or even help me pay for a funeral. You go out there and still find trouble. Have Slam ever been to my house? You know how I feel about that anyway." She looked at me.

"Nah, he haven't," I answered.

"He wants what y'all got. It's like he's all over the place right now, getting everybody into it. Box him in, he being greedy. Take the nigga out the quietest way possible. You and Derek can't get y'all hands dirty nomo. You can talk to him all day, but you don't tell your left hand what your right hand is doing. Think about it. He may be tryna take one of y'all out to become the other man's right hand. It happens, son. It's good to learn a persons history. You'll have a better understanding on why they make the moves they make. Get to know Slam. You might understand him more. It'll make sense. Even though that shit not cool, you'll understand his snake ass motive." My mom preached.

"Good looking, ma." I thanked her.

"Boy, good looking, my ass! Why this room smell like hot sex, cologne, and feet!? Let the windows up. Matter of fact, clean up, ugh!" She nagged.

I couldn't do anything but laugh when she walked out the room. I knew she wouldn't tell me anything wrong and she knows about the streets. Imma keep it real, I don't give a fuck about his motive. Nigga, you put us in danger. Imma ask him one mo' time and if the story don't sound right or if I think he missing any details, his ass over with. I don't have time to be playing with niggas. It's either you with me or you not. Ain't that much money in the world that'll make me switch up. We got one mo' lick to hit and we gon' holla at him. Right now, I know this the big one.

We played it cool for the next few days. We was on the block when Slam called me and said it was time we met him on Culver street.

"You ready?" Slam asked me and Derek as we met up.

Derek just nodded.

"Who are these niggas?" I asked Slam.

"A bunch of nobodies. Shid, y'all don't even need masks, to be honest. He knows me, so Imma put my mask on." Slam insisted.

"Man, how the fuck you sound? If you wear one, we wearing one, too. Slam, what you on? Derek asked, suspiciously.

"Nah, bro. I'm just saying," Slam said.

"Don't just say! Let's get this over with. Let us put our mask on and you keep yours off." Derek poked at him.

"That don't make sense," Slam said, confused.

"Shid, that's what we telling you," I told him, with a stale face.

The whole ride there, me and D kept quiet. Keeping everything brief with the nigga Slam. Derek wanted me to drive while he sat in the back, just in case Slam tried anything. When we pulled up, we went right in the nigga house. Nobody was there so we started grabbing everything until I heard a car pull up. I looked out the window to see a nigga walking towards the house we were in. Me and Derek instantly got on point when the nigga walked through the front door, only to find out it was Big Man's brother. This nigga Slam put us in another jam. Before Derek can even show Big Man's brother that it's him, Slam takes off through the backdoor, leaving us with Big Man's Brother. We take the masks off.

"D and Eli? Man, what the fuck y'all doing in my crib?" J yelled.

"Man, J, I swear to you, on Pops, I didn't know this was yo crib. Yo cousin, Slam, set this up." I explained.

We sat in J's front room for a while, talking and discussing things. Not once did Slam check on us. He did take off with a bag full of J's stuff, though. Slam knew we knew J. Better yet, not only are J and Big Man brothers, but J and Derek's big brother, who was killed, was best friends. So, we know this nigga personally. Slam knew that. I'ont know if it's just me he's trying to take out, or Derek. Hell, or even both of us, but we got something for him. The whole time we were at J's crib, Endia was calling. When I finally answered, of all the things she could tell me, she tells me she's pregnant. I mean I was happy, but I had a snake on my hands that I needed to get out the way. Then, I thought about what OG said. I had too much on my mind, so I told her I'll call her when I make it in. I'm still stuck on this nigga telling us we didn't need a mask when in reality, we needed more than a mask. We ain't need to be there at all. J watched after us. After we left J-dog crib, Derek stayed at my house. We needed a plan. I wanted this nigga to feel whatever we brought his way. Derek just wanted to off him, but messing with a greasy ass nigga like Slam, you had to be careful.

We hadn't seen Slam in about a week. I guess he thought we would forget. I was more ready to smoke his bitch ass than Derek was. One of us had to use our head though, and I think it was on me. We were standing in front of Derek's girl crib when Slam walked up.

"Wassup, y'all?" Slam asked us, as if nothing ever happened.

Derek looked back but didn't reply. His look said it all. Out of nowhere, I hit ass right in the jaw. All I could think about was how we held that nigga down, gave him passes, let him kick it with us , and even after Derek was iffy about him, I still gave him a chance. The minute I swung, Derek came right behind me. I knew he was waiting on that. We still gave the nigga a pass. We didn't whoop him how we could have. I grabbed Derek and we left his snake ass balled up. I know I could've went about it differently, but the fact that this nigga thought we would forget or it was cool to put us in different jams caused me to react the way I did. I'm not leaving without Derek in any situation, though. A nigga gotta kill both of us. Slam had us in a nigga, who watched us grow up and looked out for us, crib. He knows J be in and out of town. He lives in Atlanta but he's always in and outta the city. Whether he was there or not, Slam knew it was his crib and still tried to send us off, talking 'bout we didn't need a mask. Why would you want any mu'fucka to see our faces? I don't even wanna know. That nigga ain't got nothing to say to me.

My phone starts to vibrate. It was my mom.

"Wassup, Ma?" I answered.

"Help me understand why Slam called my phone saying y'all jumped on him." She stated, frantically.

"What?" I asked, in disbelief.

"WHY IS HE CALLING ME? Better yet, why does he have my number? I told you how to go about it! You let your temper take over. Now, you gotta watch yo back. I moved you from the hood to get away from this." She screamed.

"Ma, calm down. I'm not worried about him. You don't have to be worried." I stated in a calm tone.

"Alright, son. Be careful, Love you." She told me back, calming down.

"Love you too." We hung up.

With everything going on, I haven't really had time for Endia. The pregnancy threw me off a lil' bit, but I was still tryna figure some stuff out. By something, I mean everything that's been going on. I told her to meet me at my crib so we can talk . I still had to find a way to tell my mama. She already said what she said and in a sense, she was right. I still wanted to tell her. Not now, though. It's too much going on, but then again, this might be the right time.

Handle That

Chapter 5

I had a test in about three different classes, so I had to be on time and ready. One of those tests had me up all night, trying to study. In the first two classes, I was the first one done. All these sidity white boys in the class and I finished first. Before my last class, I bumped into Curt. He didn't say much. He just handed me his phone. He had a serious look on his face, like some was bothering him.

"You cool?" I asked him.

"Yeah. Here, this Big Man," he told me.

I was supposed to be at lunch, but this call was more important. I ain't talked to my boy in a while. I kind of feel bad.

"Wassup, B?" I greeted him.

"Damn Eli, you forgot about me?" He asked me, playfully.

"Man, hell nah. It's been so much going out here." I explained.

"Yeah, I know. You and Derek goof asses broke in big bro's crib." He exclaimed.

We both laughed.

"Man, that was all Slam goof ass. I think he set that shit up. Me and Derek started rocking with him right after you got booked." I told him.

"I told y'all dumb ass, and I know you ain't letting niggas in. Shid, I guess you sweet now." He joked.

"Man, hell naw. I just had to lighten up. Me and Derek couldn't both be wild, terrorizing niggas and having niggas scared. Being cool and can't forget mean. Shid, you balanced it out but when you left, I had to." I confessed.

"Man, you let my cousin jam you up. Family or not, we don't move like that. How you not seeing it and we was taught to be ahead of the player and the game. Shid, you the one taught me to think like that. Why you think I wasn't tight with my cousin when I was out? The nigga told you not to use a mask, come on now.

My cousin not right. Even if you didn't know my brother lived there, ain't no question that nigga knew." He explained to me.

"That's just the last thing. We beat his ass, though." I smirked.

"Wait, so this wasn't the first time?" He asked, shocked.

"Man, I'ont wanna talk about it. What's been up?" I tried to change the subject.

"Nothing much. When you move to the Suburbs?" He asked me, intrigued.

"Almost a year ago. Yo baby mama moved and changed numbers so fast." I told him.

"Yeah, I know and I know why she didn't call you with it." He stated.

"Then, Me and Derek got locked up and both got new numbers."

"Y'all was supposed to do that, anyway. Especially after everything that went on." He agreed.

"We was trying to keep the numbers for you, but fter we heard a beep and breathing on the phone a few times, we knew it was time then to get new numbers. I gotta get to class, though. Imma give Curt my number. Better yet, you take it," I paused until he was ready, "313-905-0875."

"Aye, before you give the phone back, who is this nigga Dave? I heard he be whooping my daughter." He told me.

"Dave? Nigga, you talking about Slam?" I asked in disbelief.

"Shid, I'ont know. My babymama's new nigga. She say it's not my cousin and my brother said the same thing . This nigga whooping my daughter, though." He said angrily.

"Only Dave I know is your cousin, the one we talked about this whole time. He never brought it up to us." I explained.

"Man, find out and handle that. Oh, I need you to stop at 1219 North Halo. Go to the basement. Thank me later." He said.

"It's gon' get done and alright." We hung up.

After getting off the phone, I knew after this, it was really it. It's like he knew what he was doing. This was one nigga I just didn't understand. Derek's brother, we used to talk about niggas like him. Me and Derek are loyal, so how we attract this nigga? Then Big Man said a ngga named Dave hitting his daughter. I'm knowing it's another Dave out there 'cause ain't no way this nigga been creeping like that. Anyway, this address sounded familiar.

I'm Trying To Get To The Bottom
Chapter 6

I did all that studying and still failed that test. I stayed up late for shit, taking all those notes. I need a tutor or something. I'm glad I'm not failing the class 'cause I would've been pissed. I still need to holla at this teacher to see where I went wrong. I didn't go to my last two classes. I needed to get up with D right away. He picked me up from school. I had him ride me past that address Big Man gave me. Once I saw the house, I didn't understand why I had to go there. I know I've seen the address before, but what was Big Man trying to tell me? It was always the loyalty, honesty, and the real in him that stuck out. That's probably why me, him, and Derek became one. No matter the situation or who it involved. It made me anxious to see what was there or who. I knew we, or even me, was gon' bend back to that house soon. Me and Derek ended up meeting the guys at the park. We talked for a minute, then who do I see? This nigga Slam, of course, but he made a U-turn 'cause he knew he wasn't welcomed. I would've gotten on the subject about Big Man, but he was already in all kinds of hot water. Plus, we was taking care of business. I'll take care of that after this.

After we left the park, I told Derek what me and Big Man talked about.

"Wait, so this nigga messing with Big Man's daughter, like putting hands on her or touching her? I don't give a fuck. Call him and I hope I'ont gotta find him." Derek fumed.

"Man, at this point, it's whatever. Then, Big Man said to go to this address and never said why." I stated, still confused.

"Call Slam and see where he at. Let's talk." Derek insisted.

I called him, but to no avail.

"He didn't answer," I told Derek.

"Man, he see you calling. That nigga know wassup." Derek nodded his head.

"We just gon' slide to his crib." I shrugged.

"The old Eli's back. That's the nigga I know. Yeaahhhhhh!" Derek yelled.

We both laughed.

"Man, I never left." I smirked.

"Shid, the only time I seen you be you was when we went to squash that shit." He laughed.

"We both can't be hot." I laughed back.

"Nigga, I kept the peace!" Derek exclaimed.

"One time." I chuckled.

"That's enough for me." He shrugged.

"Remember, I was telling you about Endia?" I asked him.

"What about her?" He furrowed his eyebrows.

"She's pregnant. I'm not mad that she's pregnant, I'm just mad at the timing. I still need to hit licks and finish any beef we got. I need to get myself together first; mentally, physically, emotionally, and financially. I don't wanna bring my baby into this world with everything that's going on, if it makes sense?" I confessed.

"Yeah, it do. Nigga, you told yo mama?" He asked, raising his eyebrows.

"Why?" I asked, skeptically.

"Shid, she gon' think it was my fault." He shook his head.

"Man, get yo scary ass!" I laughed at him.

"She knows her son is the devil and fucks like a rabbit, but still blames me. Imma give Mrs. Rose some act right. I bet she won't act up with me again, with her old, thick ass." Derek joked.

"Aye! Don't play with my Mama." I stated with all seriousness.

"Man, get yo soft, crybaby ass on." Derek laughed.

"Show me." I told him, smirking.

"Don't act like I can't, knowing I used to beat yo ass." Derek smirked back.

"Nigga, you better stop confusing me before I confuse you with another nigga." I laughed.

Derek laughed back.

"This what I gotta do for you to give yo girl or Rose back their panties." Derek said, playfully.

"Nigga, you know wassup." I said back.

We pulled up to Slam's house, but of course, he wasn't home. Then, it dawned on me. He was probably at Big Man's baby mama's house. I instantly called Curt. Low and behold, that's where he was. Dave was Slam. Guess it was time to pay our boy a visit.

When we got there, Curt let us in. We walked in and this nigga Slam almost shitted on himself when he saw us.

"How y'all-" Slam started.

Before he could get anything out, Derek stopped him.

"We not doing this here. Where is Big Man's daughter?" Derek asked him in a cold tone.

"Nyseer in the room with Shaunni." Curt blurted out.

"Wake Shaunni up. I got a good mind to beat yo ass, too." I told Curt.

"Slam, we don't give a fuck about you fucking Shaunni. Nigga, you putting yo hands on his daughter? Nigga, you probably the one told on him. That's probably why you would get mad when we brought him up or the reason you took us to his brother's crib." Derek fumed.

"Man, I didn't do nothing to his daughter." Slam pleaded.

"Let me ask her." I insisted.

"She'll say anything. She's a kid!" Slam exclaimed, loudly.

Slam started to walk off and Derek jumped at him. I thought he was gonna hit him in the jaw, but I guess he was just trying to scare him. Derek plays too much, anyway. He probably found it funny. Me, Derek and Curt stood in the dining room. Me and Derek had to have been thinking the same thing because Curt got hit from both ways. I hit him in the right jaw. Derek hit him in the left. It was like I hit him into Derek and Derek through him back.

"What y'all do that for?" Curt asked, holding his face.

"Nigga, 'cause you letting him hit yo niece. Then, this nigga a snake ass, scary ass nigga!" I answered him, loudly.

My nigga instincts told me Eli was gone do it, anyway. So, I did it, but what Eli said makes sense." Derek added.

"I didn't know he was hitting her." Curt lied.

I hit Curt again.

"Lie again!" I yelled.

"That's what I'm talking about." Derek boasted, clapping his hands.

"Ok, I knew, but Shaunni let him. What am I supposed to do? That's her baby!" Curt exclaimed.

Derek started to charge for Curt with his fist balled up.

"That's yo niece! Don't let no nigga do anything to her. You forgot Big Man beat yo daddy ass for hitting you and Shaunni when he was drunk!" Derek said, loudly.

"You scared?" I asked Curt as I walked towards him.

"Nah, Shaunni be tweaking! When I did say something, me and him got into it. Then, eventually me and her got into it. She put me out. She said it was cool. That he not gon' hurt her." Curt explained.

Shaunni is a heavy set light skinned girl with braids, a round face, dimples, and thick eyebrows with a few freckles on her face. She could still rank an 8, though.

"What's taking so long?" I asked out loud.

"First off, who invited y'all here?" Shaunni asked us as she walked into the room.

"Damn, no how we doing? If we hungry or nothing, huh?" Derek joked.

"You still crazy." Shaunni shook her head.

"I didn't come too reunite. Do this on y'all own time. I came to handle something." I stated with a serious tone.

"Mm-hm, you still rude and mean, I see." Shaunni rolled her eyes.

I gave Shaunni the meanest, nastiest look ever. If looks could kill, she would be gone.

"Hey Nyseer, you remember me?" I asked babygirl.

"Yes. You buy me cookies. Well, a long time ago." She answered, smiling.

Nyseer was about 6 years old with curly hair, a round face like Shaunni, with the same dimples as well. She was caramel. I guess as dark as Big Man is and as light as Shaunni is, she was bound to be in the middle. She also had oily skin. I can see Big Man now on her first date if he's out, with a gun letting whatever nigga know to be careful with her. I'm ready to be behind him or step in his place. Hell, I was at the hospital, birthdays, and baby shower, too. Even though I haven't seen her in a year, she remembered me.

"Look what I got you. Let me run to the car." I told Nyseer, smiling while leaving to go to the car.

"Aye, Shaunni, grab me some to drink. I am a guest. Fix me some to eat too." Derek ordered her.

"Damn, you should've ate before you came! You not a guest. Go find you something." Shaunni exclaimed, rolling her eyes.

"When you go six months or longer without communicating, I don't know you anymore." Derek stated.

"You still dramatic." She said, laughing.

"You laughing, ain't nothin' funny. With Big Man being locked up, we wanna at least help with his daughter. You changed numbers and moved out here. I had this same number for years. You know we was giving money for Big Man and whatever else. Why for this nigga Slam?" Derek asked her.

"Man, don't put me in that." Slam waved his hand.

"You said you wanna fight?" Derek turned his attention to Slam.

"I'm just saying, bro. I know we got something going on, but we not doing that here. It wasn't my fault she lost contact." Slam shrugged.

"Piss on my head and tell me it's raining, you down south motherfucker." Derek grilled him.

I walked back through the door with a big, pink and purple dollhouse and a bag full of clothes and shoes. I also had another bag with a toy car for the dolls and three more dolls.

Nyseer eyes lit up and she smiled from ear to ear. She started jumping around, excitedly.

"Are you gon' say "thank you"?" Shaunni asked Nyseer, implicating her to say thanks.

"Thank you, what's yo name again?" Nyseer asked me with a shy voice.

"Elijah, and this my number when you want anything." I told her.

"That stuff came from us." Derek joked.

They all started laughing.

"Nyseer , does he hit you?" I asked her, softly.

"Um, no." She answered as she finished playing with the dolls.

"And even if he did, that's my child. I take care of her!" Shaunni stated, loudly.

I'll Figure It Out

Chapter 7

"I wouldn't care if it was the president's daughter! Big Man said she was getting hit and I came to find out. Why is another man hitting on her, anyway?" Derek asked her, disgusted with her.

"I gave him permission, but he never did it." Shaunni told him.

"Yeah, aite. Don't get no ideas." Derek cut his eyes at both Slam and Shaunni.

"If that's it, I'll get y'all number, and we will see y'all later." Shaunni told us, rolling her eyes.

"You putting us out?" Derek asked, raising his eyebrows.

"No, but yeah," she shrugged.

Slam walked us out. We really didn't have much to talk about. Only reason we didn't whoop him again was because lil' Nyseer was there. We probably would've beat Shaunni ass, too, and smacked her a few times, by mistake though. Just in case she tried to break it up, she would've caught one. I know she told Nyseer to lie, but it'll come out like everything always does.

"See, man, I told you." Slam exclaimed.

"We ain't come to talk or kick it. I came to beat yo ass, but since it was confusion, I can't." Derek confessed.

"Wasn't no confusion. They probably made Nyseer say no." I said.

"No, but aite. Y'all be smooth." Slam told us.

"That's a threat or some?" I asked him, defensively.

"Damn bro, you actin' how Derek was actin' with me." Slam stated, shocked at how I was coming off to him.

"You showed yo true colors. All I had to do is give you a chance and didn't even have to do that." I told her, looking at him in disgust.

"It's just been too much going on. It seems like I been doing wrong, but it's not like-" Slam tried to explain.

"Aye, we didn't come to reunite." Derek cut him off.

Me and Derek got in the car and pulled off, leaving Slam standing there.

"Why couldn't we whoop him? You know he was lying." Derek fumed.

"You not using yo head. Big Man's baby girl was there. We could traumatize or scare her. We don't do that. We gone get him, just be patient." I explained to him.

"That meeting still on today with TB and his people about these blocks?" Derek asked me, switching the subject.

"Yeah." I answered.

It's Time

Chapter 8

See, Slam never knew we squashed what we had with TB and his guys, which is the niggas he claimed shot at him for nothing. We meet in the park at 8:50 pm. I got time to introduce my mama to my girl. It was only 3 pm, so I had enough time. I had D to drop me off at home.

"Damn, I wasn't invited to family time?" Derek joked.

"Same nigga that was scared to pull in front of the crib last week." I joked back.

"I wasn't. I just didn't wanna get into it with yo mama other boyfriend." He smirked.

"Right!" I rolled my eyes.

"I'm cool, Rose might not want you in our business, anyway. You don't know Imma be Stepdaddy pretty soon." Derek chuckled.

"We haven't went to the backyard in a long time. I would hate to whoop you real quick." I told him.

"Don't forget who won last." He reminded me.

"Nigga, it don't matter! As long as you feel this left and right. I got you way more than you got me." I blasted.

"I wasn't ready." Derek laughed.

"Right!"

"Who car parked in our driveway?" Derek asked, continuing to play.

"That's Endia's car, but why she here?" I asked to myself.

"And Rose here." Derek stated.

"So much for dinner at 8 and to talk." I shook my head.

"Right, she met Rose before?" Derek asked.

"They seen each other before but not really." I shrugged.

"Well' let me know how it go. I have to run Grandma to the grocery store and help her clean up for the BBQ tomorrow." Derek stated, starting the car up.

"I'll be over. You already know." I smiled.

"Alright. Love, bro." Derek told me, as we shook up.

"Love."

As I walked to the door, I was trying to think of what was being said on the other side. Endia was the type to let you know about her, even when you didn't ask. She was pretty bold and outspoken. So, I'm pretty sure she introduced herself. The question is how did my mama take it. My mama was the same way but an older version. My mama was more aggressive, though. I'm picturing how this could've went...

Endia: Hey, I'm Endia.

Ma: I'm Rose. Who are you looking for?

Endia: I'm introducing myself to you. I'm Elijah's girlfriend.

Ma: And where is he?

Endia: I'm not sure, but I came to meet you myself.

Ma: Why is that? This my off day. I didn't plan on being bothered with my son or his lil' girlfriend, that took it upon herself to meet me.

Endia: Well, you're gonna be a grandma and since he's been busy in the streets, I thought I'd come talk to you myself, but I'll let him deal with it.

Ma: You should've done that in the first place. You don't know me and I don't know you.

…I'm pretty sure it went something like that. I told my mama about Endia, but I didn't tell her she was pregnant. Especially not with everything going on. She would have a fit and I didn't have time for it. As I put my key in the door, my mama opened it.

"Congratulations on your first born that I had to find out about from a girl you told me about, that I only seen once but met without you." She whispered, sarcastically while smiling.

I started to laugh because I knew she would say that or something similar. I hugged her and as she hugged me back, she said, "You better be lucky I like her."

The minute I walked in, I hugged Endia. If I'm lying, I'm dying, Endia said the same thing, "Oh Elijah, thanks for telling yo mama about the baby."

I couldn't do nothing but laugh. They remind me of a younger and older version of each other. I don't know what I got myself into. My mama was showing Endia pictures of me and planning the baby shower for her. She seemed excited to me. Endia not even 6 weeks, but I wasn't gon' tell them that they was talking about a baby shower too early. I just went with the flow. Endia came across a picture with me and my dad.

"This him?" She asked.

"Yeah," I smiled, slyly.

"You can't tell with that funny looking ass face.?" My mama joked.

We all laughed and talked until my phone started to ring back to back.

"Elijah, who is that?" Endia asked me. I can hear the attitude in her voice.

"Man, I don't know. I'm tryna enjoy time with y'all. Is that a problem?" I asked back, holding my arms out.

"Yeah, when somebody is blowing up your phone and you can't answer it. Mm-hm, must be a female or something." Endia rolled her eyes at me.

"I remember those days." My mama laughed at us.

"I got 2 messages and 16 missed calls and I'm pretty sure they all from the guys." I explained.

"Better be!" Endia exclaimed.

"Man, watch out! These from D. He outside, so I gotta go." I told her.

"You said we was gon' spend time." Endia whined.

"You stay here until I get back and I'll stay in tomorrow with you." I promised her, getting up to leave.

As I walked out to the car, D was walking up to me.

"Family time over since you didn't answer. Thought y'all was having so much fun, but let's get to the meeting before we lose these niggas." Derek said.

About twenty minutes later, we pulled up to the park. It was at least 30 niggas out, 15 from each side. When me and Derek got out, TB clapped and said finally. As the meeting began, we all agreed to squash any bad beef and just get money. We got this little oath that we all abide by. What we didn't know was, we had a secret watcher. With all the guns we had, we still lacked. He didn't try nothing, but he saw us. One of the lil' shorties, Coby, saw him walking fast coming from the park as he was walking to it. The minute the shorty got there, he asked, "Why Slam leave?" We was all confused, but he told us he saw him leaving. It was kind of funny how the same nigga you try to get us into it with, we squashed beef and get money with now. Pretty sure it messed his understanding up. After the meeting, I had Derek drop me back off at home. It made me happy to walk in and see my mama and my girl in the same room, kicking it.

"Glad you can make it." My mom said, sarcastically.

"Yeah, me too. What we eating?" I asked, excitedly.

"We ate. Should've ate when you was out." She stated.

"Y'all didn't leave me nothing?" I asked in disbelief.

"We didn't know how long you planned on staying out. You know how you do." She rolled her eyes.

"Either y'all left me something or not." I said, getting irritated.

"It's some left in the kitchen." Endia butted in.

"I wouldn't have said nothing. He should've seen if we ate something while he was out." My mama said to her.

My mama boyfriend came in. He was light skinned with a beard, a bald head, and dark brown eyes.

Kind of nigga that worked out just to show he had muscles.

Like I said, the nigga was cool, but that was it. We kicked it, but I didn't want him thinking he was Pops. I had to remind him without reminding him. Every time we started to bond, I fell back. He a good nigga. Bought my mama the house we in, take care of the kids and grandkids, treat my mama right, and get her whatever she wants. Even when I remind the nigga he not my daddy, he still comes through. Whether I'm in a jam in the streets or at home. Hell, he bonded me out for $1,500 after I told the nigga me and my mama didn't need him. That still didn't stop him from coming through. My mama swore she didn't ask him for the money for my bond. So, that kind of made me realize he was actually there for me. I'll never forget the time my mama found a gun hidden in the bathroom closet, behind the towels. She was talking about putting me out and everything. Instead, he took the fall and got put out the house for three days and slept on the couch the other two. He's been around for so long. I'll also never forget when I was having a nightmare about something Me and Derek did. It was nothing major. We was robbing an old man and he put his hands up, but I thought he tried to take Derek's gun. My first reaction was to shoot him before he shot one of us. When I realized what he was actually doing, I felt bad but I couldn't keep him alive either. So, I had to finish him. He begged and swore he wouldn't go to the police, but I couldn't take that chance. When he held his hands up, he held them in front of him, so I thought he was reaching. I was wrong, but what really had me was when I opened his wallet and saw a family picture. A few days later, I saw his family on the news. To see his son cry, it made me feel worse 'cause I know that pain.

Anyway, my mama boyfriend heard me sleep one night and woke me up. It's like he already knew, so we didn't say much. We just sat quietly for three minutes. He broke the silence and told me "You can't be hot headed about everything. No matter what you're doing, it's okay to think it out and be smooth. Being hot headed, you are begging for attention. Real niggas, real killers, and real hustlers move in silence. Talking get you caught. I know what you did and I'm not saying it to hold it over yo head, tell yo mama, or the police. I'm letting you know next time, move better. You wouldn't be having these nightmares. All I'm saying is, you taking from a person is enough, but taking a person from their family is something else. You know how it feel." After that day, he was cool in my book. I mean, he still wasn't my pops, but he would do for now. Now that I think about it, that incident with the old man was major while I'm talking about it not being major. My mama boyfriend wanted a bond so bad, but I was being stubborn when I didn't have to. He had one foot in the streets and one foot out. He still had a name in the streets, even though he went from a "street nigga" to a "business man" in a matter of time. I eventually wanted to do the same. He had a building and sold cars. He turned his drug money into something better. He told me he was never a killer, but a smooth, quiet money-getter. The streets became too risky and he knew once he had kids, he couldn't keep risking his life for hating ass niggas or a messed up system. So, he had to find a better way to make money and that way was owning buildings and renting them.

My Brother
Chapter 9

When he walked in the house with us, he had this sad, lost look on his face. When he seen me, the nigga eyes lit up and he ran to hug me.

"You cool?" I asked him, confused.

"Right, what the hell wrong with you?" My mom asked, also confused.

"Man, I thought that was you laid out on Truth street." Her boyfriend confessed.

"Aw, I been here for a minute now. I didn't hear nothing about it, though." I furrowed my eyebrows.

"Man, I'm glad you cool." He breathed deeply.

"Hell, he better be and the bastard got a baby on the way." My mom teased.

"Aw yeah? You must be the lucky young lady. I'm Alex." He greeted Endia, smiling.

"Yeah, my bad. This is my girl, Endia. This Alex, my pops." I introduced them.

My mama and Alex both were surprised. I can tell by their facial expressions. It's like we said something to each other without saying anything. To know he was actually hurt when he thought it was me laid out, did something to me. Even from him just being there for me overall. I didn't try to say pops, but it came out and I let it. We both know he's not my daddy, but it's time to start appreciating him more and showing it. This nigga acted like he was ready to cry when I introduced him as my pops. His ass is still a corn ball.

In the process of all that, from the time I got to the house, my phone was on silent. So, my mama phone rang. She listened to whoever was on the other end of the phone and started to scream. Me and Alex ran over to her.

"It's Derek!" She screamed.

I stepped back and picked my phone up. I had at least 20 missed calls. My mama tried hugging me, but I dodged it. With no shoes on, I ran out the front door. Endia screamed out for me to come back, but I kept going. Without missing a beat, Alex pulled up on the side of me. I jumped in and we sped to Derek's house. When we got there, everybody was in front of his house. I heard his grandma screaming.

"Where is Elijah!? My baby needs him!"

"I'm right here. Where is D? What happened? Who did this?" I asked, frantically.

"Where were you when they shot my baby? You know you don't leave his side. How did you let this happen, Elijah? Get that bastard! Derek is all I have. God, please! An old lady like me can't take this heartache. Please have mercy!" Derek's grandma cried out.

I checked my missed calls again. My brother called six times. My head was everywhere. I was ready for whatever with whoever. If my brother doesn't make it, I'm painting the city red! Anybody he ever exchanged harsh words with or anybody whoever looked at him funny. Anything! I'm making sure them niggas feel my pain. So, they better pray long and hard. I rushed to the hospital. When I got there, they didn't have any updates for me. I had never prayed to God so hard, but I did this night. Derek, my brother. You barely see one without the other. We big on loyalty. I cried with and in front of him. He's more than a friend. We're family. Why come after him? Why not me? He's the goofy and playful one. I'm the one who's mean and doesn't really joke with people. I'm tryna figure out what I do to deserve this pain. My pops, Derek's brother, Big Man. A nigga I let in my circle snaked me, and now Derek. I lost others, but this hurt the most. This was family! The images came running through my head. My mama boyfriend stayed with me the whole time. Every few minutes, I was walking up to the doctors, asking questions. I was ready to shoot every doctor that couldn't give me an answer. I walked off to go to the vending machine. When I walked in the vending machine room, between the chairs, I heard crying. It was my lil' homie, Coby. The same one me and Derek called our little brother, the same one who saw Slam walking away from the meeting that he was never at. I broke down right with him. The fact that I had missed calls from Derek is eating me up 'cause he needed me and I wasn't there. I'm not leaving this place.

Missing Pieces
Chapter 10

"How you get here?" I asked Coby.

"I rode in the ambulance." He told me.

"How did you know or hear about it?" I questioned him.

"I was right there. I heard and saw everything." He confessed.

Coby was about thirteen years old. He wanted to run with me and Derek so bad, but we couldn't let him go down the same road we went down. He was a good kid. He was just lost. He pretty much raised himself. He started hustling at an early age. His mama not on drugs or anything. She's just busy trying to please whatever man she comes across. It's been times where she would feed a man before her own son. How do I know? Because Derek's brother got on her about that before he passed. I see it didn't make much of a difference, though. If them niggas wasn't tryna beat her, they was tryna beat him. Only because he tried to help her. We try keeping him on the right track, but how can we if we are doing wrong ourselves? It's all about leading by example.

"What you mean you heard and seen everything?" I asked him, angrily.

"I was right there looking out the window. I called you." He stated in a sad tone.

I broke down again 'cause I wasn't supposed to miss no calls.

"Who house was you at? Break it down. Did you hear what they was saying?" I asked through my tears.

"I was playing the game and heard Derek ask somebody "Why you here?" I thought he was talking to a female. So, I got up and looked, and saw it was Slam. Slam asked if they could talk after Derek asked why he was there. I guess D was in a good mood 'cause he let Slam talk. D saw me looking, but Slam didn't. I wasn't trying to be seen, either. But anyway...

Derek: Wassup? Why you here?

Slam: I wanna holla at you about the meeting earlier.

Derek: Ain't nothin' to talk about. I'm trying not to whoop you. Granny still woke, and she don't need that right now.

Slam: I wanna apologize. I'm bogus for everything. I know you might not forgive me, but I don't want no bad blood between us. The meeting was about me, wasn't it?

Derek: Man, I'm not tryna hear that. Gone while I'm letting you walk away.

Slam: Man, nigga, I'm tryna make things right.

"Derek stood up. I knew he was ready to fight or shoot Slam. I saw it all in his face. Slam cleared the confusion up fast." Coby continued.

Slam: My bad, bro. Let's walk down. I know yo Grandma in there. I don't wanna disturb her.

Derek: You not because you gone lower yo voice.

Slam: I'm just saying I don't want us beefing. I know you never liked me and that's cool. It's over. We don't have to speak again. I just don't want either one of us watching over our shoulders.

Derek: That's a threat?

Slam: What? Nah, it's not. I'm just saying.

"Derek was still standing up with his arms crossed. His grandma opened the door." Coby went on.

Derek's grandma: Derek, I need you to clean this house before we leave for the grocery store and my doctor's appointment in the morning. Slam, baby, where you been?

Slam: Hey, Granny. I've been around.

Derek: Alright, Granny. I'm gone clean up when I finish out here.

Granny: Alright, baby. Y'all hurry up. It's late and these fools act crazy in the summer.

Derek: Aye, we gon' walk down. Let's speed this up, too.

"Eli, man, the minute they walked down, somebody came walking out the gangway. By this time, I'm looking at the other side. Dude walked up shooting. Derek tried to up his gun and Slam shot him. He was getting it from both ways. They shot him at least seven times. I ran out when they ran off. Derek's grandma ran out, yelling his name. I yelled out for her to call you. Elijah, she broke down, begging God. Everybody was out. He picked his phone up and tried calling you. We all did. We needed you, bro. If you would've just let me get a gun, I could've shot at them niggas. Derek is my brother, too. He fed me and gave me clothes. Why Slam do it? Why he set him up? If he don't make it, I swear I'm getting Slam myself. Man, fuck that I'm getting Slam just because ain't nomo passes." Coby cried.

We both broke down. My mama came in and she felt my pain. She always knew how to hold me. I was ready to kill anybody.

"It's gonna be okay, son. We putting this in Gods' hands. Derek a fighter. He's strong. Believe in God and he'll show you." She whispered to me.

"That's my brother. I was supposed to have his back." I cried out.

"This my fault. I should've been out there, even if I couldn't do nothing." Coby cried harder.

I wiped my face and hugged lil' bro tighter.

"I can't lose both of y'all. I'm glad you was able to tell the story. I know you would have shot them niggas. I just couldn't risk you going down the wrong path. You watched us enough." I said, sadly.

"Man, fuck that, I got y'all back! I've always had it! You know it's whatever with me. Anybody can get it." Coby stated.

Listening to Coby, he reminded me so much of myself. He wasn't lying. He always had our back. One time, me and Derek had a gun on us and the police tried to get us. They didn't even have a reason. We ran and Derek threw the gun. I kid you not, Coby was on his bike watching the whole thing go down. The minute the police went past, he ran into the yard that Derek tossed the gun in and hid it. We thought we was down one gun. He could've kept it, sold it or anything, but Coby gave it back. Couldn't nobody speak on me or Derek around him because he was letting them know up front what they wasn't gon' do or say. He was a lil' nigga with a lion heart. He's always wanted to roll with us. We made sure he went to school, even when he didn't want to. Him and Derek were closer. They lived right next door to each other. Derek's grandma used to look after Coby when his dad would be drunk and beating his mother.

"Okay, baby, I know you mad, upset and hurt. I understand, but if you don't watch yo motherfuckin' mouth talking about, "Man fuck that."'" My mom told Coby.

"Sorry, Ms. Rose." Coby apologized.

"Yeah, I know. I didn't knock you upside yo head yet 'cause I know y'all hurting. He gone be fine. Just pray. God understands the bond y'all have and He wouldn't put nothing on y'all that y'all can't handle." My mom preached.

"Aye, Ma, I need to run somewhere real quick. I'll be back." I told her.

"Elijah, just please stay here. It's too hot and too much going on right now. The police are waiting on you to make a move." She pleaded.

"Ma, I'll be cool. Just keep this lil' nigga in yo sight." I pointed at Coby.

"Oh, I will!" She stated.

"Man, hel….I almost said it." Coby caught himself from cursing in front of my mom again.

"Hell. You did say it. You might as well finish. You missed an "L"and a "Naw". She laughed.

We all laughed.

"Elijah, baby, you gone do what you want, but you need to be here when Derek wakes up. He's gonna want to see you. He needs you more than you know or think. Both of y'all! Coby, you the little brother they never had, even though you got other siblings. Derek's only brother was killed, and Elijah is the only child. Where Slam at. anyway? Does he know?" My mom asked, not knowing what actually happened.

"Does he know? Yeah, he was the first to know." Coby said, sarcastically.

"We need to let the police know." My mom exclaimed.

"Man, we not telling no police. This the field, Ms. Rose." He told her with a stale face.

"Lil' boy, was I talking to you? That's the best way to go. Y'all hands don't need to be dirty." She explained.

"Well, what goes on in the streets, stays in the streets. Imma be cool, though, Ma." I told her.

"Coby, what about you?" She asked him.

"Okay, I'll stay until he wakes up, but I'm not tellin no police." Coby stood on that.

"Elijah, talk to this lil' boy before I beat him."

We waited hours. His heart stopped, but they brought him back. I don't even think I went to sleep. I couldn't! The next morning, the doctor came out with his head down.

"Family of Derek Smith." He called out.

We all stood up.

His grandmother answered, "Yes. How is he?"

"Well, I have good and bad news." He stated.

I stepped closer.

"I'm listening." I told him.

"Good news, he's still with us. Bad news, he paralyzed." The doctor stated with a sorrowful tone.

"Can we see him?" I hopefully asked.

"Yeah, can we?" Coby asked behind me.

"Not just yet." The doctor stated.

"Thank you, Father. I know you heard my cries and prayers." Derek's grandma cried out.

"What I tell y'all?" My mama said to us, smiling.

I broke down again. I wanted my brother fully back. My mama's boyfriend could've been left, but he stayed the whole time. I can't believe this. My brother, my best friend, can't walk. He had it on him, so I know they would've had a shootout. 'Cause Derek wasn't going. Slam set that up real good, but I got something

better for my boy, Slam. I gotta handle this myself!
Bringing him around was my fault. Imma solve my
problem. It won't reverse what happened, but Slam
would be out the way. Pretty sure I'm next. See, Slam
was so concerned about the meeting we had, the nigga
was scared. He thought it was about him when in
reality, it was about money. He knew he had to get us
before we got him, but what he don't know is, I'm
coming for mine. When I catch him, he must die! Me
and Derek are one. When he hurts, I feel it ten times
worse. My mama took Endia home. I called her to give
an update. I sat at the hospital all day. When he opened
his eyes, I was there. We both shed tears and he
squeezed my hand so tight. I didn't know what it meant,
but I squeezed his hand back even tighter.

"My brother forever, I'll always be here. I'm
sorry I didn't answer. You wouldn't be like this." I told
him.

I started to cry. He grabbed my hand and put his
other hand on my heart. I don't know what I would've
done if I lost him. This was more than a brotherly bond.
This ain't no ordinary friendship. Now that he's woke, I
thought I would be able to leave, but a tear fell from his
eyes when I walked off. Mine instantly started
dropping. Coby walked in.

"Man, I know y'all soft ass not crying! Nigga, I
knew you was gone make it." Coby smiled.

I laughed and Derek smiled. Derek couldn't
talk, but we understood.

"D, you should've seen Coby in the vending
machine room crying, and he cursed in front of Rose!
She was about to beat his ass." I told Derek, teasing
Coby.

"I'm not worried about yo mama." Coby
laughed.

"Yeah, I know." I smirked.

Derek's eyes grew wide. Guess who was at the door. It was like Slam was asking me to get him. This nigga popped up with flowers and a card. I'm tryna figure out what he thought he was doing. I was shocked that this nigga had the nerve to show his face here. Before I can react, I see the flowers fly in the air. Coby was beating the man nonstop. Not only was Security there, but this nigga brought the police with him. I'm assuming he was trying to see if he was dead or what condition he was in.

Of course, they locked Coby up for 8 hours. Coby wouldn't tell them why he did that, so it brought attention to everyone. The police started questioning everybody. We all kept our mouths sealed. I meant what I said, "Slam gon' feel my pain." The fact that he even stepped in this room, lets me know he takes me for some type of joke. Derek said the same thing a few weeks ago, too. I had Derek's grandma put a restriction on the room.

When they let Coby out, this lil' nigga swore he did major time. Get that lil' ass 8 hours out of here. I knew I would catch Slam. I wanted to get him before he caught any of my people. Big Man called. I'm tryna figure out how does he know what happened. He kept it real brief.

"Keep y'all heads up out there. We come from the worse part of town. Tell Derek, "He's too strong to fold." I heard y'all went to the crib, disturbing the peace. It's cool. Good looking. Elijah, I need you to go to that address. You gon' thank me later." He told me.

"Alright, what's the reason you keep telling me, though?" I asked him.

"I don't like talking on these phones, but it'll make sense. Look for the phone. Blood makes you related, loyalty made us family. Remember that."

The phone hung up. The next few days, Endia and my mama wanted me close. I just let everything die down. My mama agreed to let Coby stay for a few days. It was too risky. Coby was ready for whatever and down for whatever. Hadn't nobody seen Slam. Not even Curt. I prayed last night that I found him and in the middle of my prayer, my life changed. My boy was gone.

"God, how could you take him? Derek, how could you leave?" I cried out.

What I heard made it hard for me to breathe. I thought he was doing good. I was confused. I didn't understand. We prayed long and hard. He held my hand. How could he leave me out here? How could he leave his grandma? He was all she had left. His brother was killed, his mama was gone, and her family stayed far. Derek was her baby. He was my partner. I guess this is the pain Derek's big brother felt when my pops was killed. My mama couldn't hug me this time. She knew what time it was. God didn't hear me. I know we made mistakes, but this hurt.

I laid on Endia and cried. She was there the whole time, this past week especially. Not even an hour later, here comes Coby, calling me. I had to answer that call right away. He was cool, but his voice sounded funny. He didn't sound like himself.

I went to meet him on the other side of town. He was in somebody's house. I never knew him to have family over here, so I was tryna see who was here. I had my gun ready, though. I was on point and couldn't trust nobody. The door was cracked. I called his name. He answered from the dining room. When I walked in,

Slam was laying on the floor. Coby caught him. I just wish it was me that caught him first. Coby was in shock. Slam was still alive. The minute I noticed him moving, I finished him. Coby had followed him here. When Slam opened the door, Coby shot him. So much for a childhood. Once you're exposed to a certain lifestyle, there's no turning back.

Snakes Don't Belong

Chapter 11

"I wanted to kill him, but I needed to save the rest for you. D in the hospital and won't ever walk again. And this nigga was still enjoying life." Coby fumed.

"He didn't make it, Coby. They called right before you called me. Derek didn't make it." I said with a sad tone.

Slam dead now! Coby shot him in his legs and back to keep him down until I came. I gave him all face shots. Ain't no surviving that. Even after the face shots, Coby stood up and shot every bullet that was left in the gun, into Slam's already dead body. I couldn't let him break down right there. I set the house on fire and we ran. That was the end of Slam. I didn't feel no better. My brother was still gone, but I was glad I didn't have to watch my back anymore. His ass didn't deserve to live, anyway. We made it back to my house to find my mama still woke. That was the last thing I wanted to deal with. I never know what'll come out her mouth. She had the news on pause while sitting on the couch, drinking coffee. I told Coby to go upstairs.

"This fire on the news..this you?" She asked me with a straight face.

"What fire? I just picked Coby up." I lied.

"It's a fire out south and they found a body. I asked you was that you. I need to know when you dot this door. It's too much going on. Y'all come walking in this house late morning. Coby, bring yo ass downstairs NOW!" She yelled.

"Come on, Ma, he's tired. He couldn't sleep at his house." I lied again.

"Why did he go home?" She asked, skeptically.

"If I knew, I could answer. It won't happen again as far as the time of night." I promised her.

"Thank you. Now tell me about the fire." She insisted.

"I can't tell you about something I don't know about." I shrugged.

"Elijah, get out my face. I don't need no police kicking my door in." She stated.

"Yeah, okay."

"Now, go and get some rest." She told me.

When I walked off, the tears started to flow. I couldn't stop picturing memories. I couldn't stop picturing him. He held my hand tight. My brother needed me. I needed him. We needed each other. I watched Coby asleep in the guest room. He tossed and turned. He witnessed D's murder and he called me. I couldn't believe it. This is what we tried to keep him away from. We showed him love, but Derek showed it more. They connected way better and they related more. I never wanted this life for Coby. I remember when Derek punched Coby up. We saw him out kicking it one day when he was supposed to be at school. Derek walked up and asked him why wasn't he in school. Coby showed Derek his report card and said "Fuck school! I'm hustling now." Derek punched Coby so hard in the jaw, he knocked his ass to the left. They started fighting. I sat down and watched it play out. Derek was right, so I didn't get in it. After that day, he started doing better in school. Coby didn't talk to Derek for almost a week, but he talked to me. We were still cool. We had to help him understand how important things were. The streets were very dangerous. We showed tough love, but he started to get the picture. I know Derek wasn't ready. I won't allow that to even be in my head. He wanted to get Coby and his grandma out of the hood. We were just misguided. That's why we went so hard for Coby. It's true what they say, "You live by the streets, you die by the streets." What I didn't understand was why couldn't he get another chance or why couldn't he just stay paralyzed? If I never felt karma before, I feel it now more than ever. What goes around, comes around. I couldn't think straight. He was all his grandma had left. He was the only brother I had. Shooting Slam and setting him on fire wasn't enough. Why was I still mad? I know why. My brother was gone. I had hell in me. I needed to release some anger. I felt all over the place. I needed to get that under control. I have to keep my head on straight, no matter what pain I'm feeling. I had people I had to look after. Derek wouldn't want this. He got his lick back. Now, it's time to get myself together. I got a baby on the way. I got my mama, Coby, and Derek's grandma to look after now. I can't fail. I already failed my brother by not being there. My plan is to get myself together, and make Derek and the people around me happy. This was a big change for me. My phone started to buzz. It was Big Man. I wasn't sure if I wanted to answer or not, but I did, anyway. He asked and said some things, "Keep y'all heads up." He also told me that I gotta go harder, stay up, stay on track, and go to that address. The last thing he said was, "You'll find the nigga that put me in jail, paid my babymama to stay away and have no contact with you, and last but not least, the reason yo mama had to be a single parent so early. I told you before, it'll all make sense. Remember, blood makes you related and loyalty makes you family. Never forget. We wasn't blood, but we was MOST DEFINITELY family."

After Big Man hung up, I said the address out loud, trying to remember it. It was on my mind more than ever now. I went and laid back down with Endia. She held me tighter. I didn't cry. I just laid there and allowed her to fall back to sleep while I rubbed her stomach, thinking about the future. I had one more thing to do, then I was done with this life. I was gon' do things right. I prayed long and hard on me finding my dad's killer and Big Man had information. It could be false, but he had evidence. So, that was a chance I was willing to take. My whole life, I prayed on that. I want out of this life due to the fact it's only left me with a million questions, and it took my brother and father from me. Big Man was locked up. I fought case after case, running from the police, and being hated on by a nigga I thought was my homie, who also took lil' Coby's street innocence. The streets left me with a heavy heart. Once I get Pops killer out the way, that's it. No more of this.

I was around Derek's family most of the day. Endia, Coby, and my mom came with me. I was there physically, but mentally, I was on another level. We left around 7 pm. I dropped them off at the house and kept going. Didn't have time for questions.

Last Snake Standing
Chapter 12

On my way there, I had all kinds of thoughts. What if it's a set up? What if jail turned Big Man into another Slam? What if my pop's killer ends up being my killer? What if I don't make it home tonight? I wanted to turn around, but this is what I prayed for. Now, the time is here. No more what if's. It was time to finish the last of this street life. For nineteen years, I woke up out of my sleep in sweats around my pop's death anniversary. Now, I could sleep peacefully. I had built up anger, and I was ready to release it on the nigga that split my family up. I said if I found his killer "He must die." When I pulled up to the house, I knew it looked familiar. I was so sick of surprises. I know Big Man playing. I just know I'm getting punked. It's always the ones who you least expect. I picked the lock and walked in the house. All the lights were out. Nobody was home. It was just how I remembered. The basement had those stairs you see on TV. Every time I walked down one, it squeaked. Once I got down there, I pulled a string to turn the light on. I was ready to shoot anything that popped out. Part of me wanted to walk out, but the other part wanted answers. Tears started to fall, but those turned into anger and the old me came out. I wondered how my life could've been with Pops around. I started to look for everything Big Man told me to look for. I wonder if he knew my pops killer was not only the one who had him locked up, but was also Slam's cousin. None of this made sense. It didn't add up. Listening to the recording was proof. This nigga was a snake! Why didn't Big Man tell me this before? What was he waiting on? Why was he waiting? I'm looking at pictures and articles, all about my pops. How can you show up to a funeral knowing you killed the one in the casket? I hated this nigga. There were statements of him telling on his brother and everything. I heard the door open and if I knew him, he already had his gun ready. So, I'm making sure he ain't getting me first. I hid. When he came down the stairs, I shot him in the leg and both arms. I didn't want him dead. I needed answers first. He sent Slam for us, but why? He hurt me five different times. Why? He took two people from me, sent Slam to snake me, set me up, killed Derek, and got Big Man locked up. Death was calling him, and I was answering that call. When I heard him fall, I jumped out so he could see me. What I didn't know was that he was gon' have a chance to hit me in the leg. His eyes bucked when he saw it was me. I didn't feel no sympathy either.

"Wassup, Eli? If you gon' kill me, then do it!" He spat.

"If I wanted you dead, you would be. I want answers."

"You might as well kill me." He said, wincing from pain.

BANG BANG! I shot him in his hand.

"I said I wanted answers! You gon' feel the pain I felt. I'm gon' start 1 by 1. Why you kill my daddy? I thought yall was friends. Why did you send Slam our way? Why did you get yo own brother locked up?" I threw questions at it.

"So, you know a lot?" He asked with a smug grin on his face.

"I know enough. Now, I'm listening."

"You left out Derek's brother." He smirked.

"What about him?" I asked, confused.

"That was all me, too. Now, him and Derek back together. It was supposed to have been you too, but that's what happens when you send a rookie." He rolled his eyes.

"I need a better understanding of what you mean." I stated, dumbfounded.

"Just like ya pops. Always needed clarity, always had bitches, always had a solid team behind him, always was loved, always well respected, and had niggas scared without even doing anything. Then, there's Derek's brother. He was just like ya old man. Always had his back. That's why I made sure that nigga was next. Then, here come you and Derek, just like them. I tried training Big Man to be like me and take niggas like you out the way. Instead, this nigga wanted to jump on the bandwagon with you. I was supposed to run that show back then. I put real work in, watching out for police sunup to sundown. Finding licks, for them to go find something better and make me look bad. Tried building a family, but had a miscarriage, then to find out you made it. And last but not least, from the crackheads to the young and old heads, they loved yo daddy. This punk ass nigga gave back to the same community he robbed. I begged yo mama for time, but she gave it to him. Some niggas don't deserve to live. I watched blocks for years, just for this nigga to wake up and run three different joints. He was living his best life while I was putting in all the work. He had everything I wanted, so he had to go. I set his ass up the same way Slam did yo homeboy Derek. Thought Derek was smarter than that. Then, here comes Derek's brother tryna put pieces together. I killed that nigga, and even carried the casket and told his mama I'll find them niggas that did it. I took you and Derek in under me, but y'all was too much like yo daddy and his brother. I rebuilt this hood. I wasn't gon' let no lil' niggas take it. My brother wanted to ride with y'all, but I'm his blood. I told him what I did and how we wasn't gon' let you take over how yo daddy did and even if he had to kill you, then do it. This bitch ass brother of mine told me "NO!" Nigga, what the fuck you mean NO!? I'm yo blood, you ride with me!" J ranted.

"So, I'm confused. You mad 'cause they wasn't snakes, was real, knew how to get money, well respected without putting in work, and ready for whatever? You just confused me. Then, you said yo brother was like us? Nigga, you the hating ass problem! You just as bad as Slam. We all supposed to be family.

Instead, you wanna be a hating, greedy nigga. Me, Derek, and Big Man ate together and split everything. How it's supposed to be. You went against yo brother and got him doing Fed time. Do his babymama even know Slam y'all cousin? You killed my pops 'cause you wanted to be him." I said in disbelief.

J smiled mischievously, knowing he hit me where it hurt and didn't feel bad for his wrongdoings, that he felt was right.

"I took everything and everybody from you. Yo daddy should've stayed in a lil' nigga's place. Nigga thought he was so tough, robbing and shooting. Thought he was getting so much money that he could help the community, ol' Robinhood ass nigga. It took me years to run the block. He comes around and in a matter of months, he's running three different blocks. It's like he jumped from Freshman to Senior. I couldn't have kids. So, yo daddy son became mine," he smirked, "Yet, you still couldn't follow the rules. Now, you fatherless and friendless. You gon' get with the program and join my team or kill me. We wasting time."

BOOM! BOOM! BOOM! BOOM! I gave him a mouth shot, two chest shots and another leg shot. I can never see myself hating on the next person so much to even kill them. The fact he found it funny and he did all of this or even told me I was gon' join his team, let me know he wasn't right. When he said I became his son, it sent me over the edge. I thought he was tryna guide me, have my back, and be there because my pops couldn't. Instead, he had his own plans. I didn't move, though. I just stood there in deep thought. Now, I understood what Big Man meant when he said, "Blood makes you related, Loyalty makes you family". I just don't understand why he didn't tell me right away. I could've been killed him. I heard footsteps, but I didn't run or hide. I stood there as a scared, lost face came creeping down the stairs. Guess who it was...lil' Coby.

"Damn!!!" He yelled.

BOOM! BOOM! Coby put two more into J.

"I missed this other snake ass nigga." Coby spat.

"How you find me?" I asked him.

"I heard you on the phone when I was half asleep. Man, why they keep doing you like this? Why they wanna hurt you so bad?" He asked me with a sad tone.

"Let's get out of here. This not the place." I told him.

We grabbed all the evidence and I was surprised the police wasn't waiting on us outside. We left and I started having flashbacks of everything. The whole ride was silent. We stopped at the hospital due to me being shot in the leg. We were in and out surprisingly. The whole ride was pretty quiet.

I prayed and got everything I prayed for. I still didn't feel no better. I found my pop's killer, and his killer was somebody that was supposed to be his brother. That hurt me way more to know it came from somebody close. The fact that he wanted to have power over the hood so bad, he went against his own. What kills me the most is that he came for me. When my plan was never to take over the hood. My plan was to have a lil' fun and eventually do the right thing. He used Slam as bait to get to me. What he didn't understand was he could've had the streets. He thought I wanted this and I didn't. This was never my plan, to go against a nigga I thought was family.

We pulled up to the house, and everything started to replay in my mind. I got so mad, I wanted to go back and shoot the nigga again. Before we got out, Coby looked at me.

"Why he do it?" He asked.

"I'll never understand his ways." I answered him, sighing deeply.

"Well, I still got yo back." He assured me with a sly smile.

I started thinking and it made sense. The day before Big Man got locked up, he told me he had something important to talk about. The next day, before he could get a chance to, the feds picked him up. When he said the other day I'll find out who wrote a statement and told on him, it was his brother. His brother knew he would tell me. I guess he had some kind of heart, though. He didn't kill him. He just set him up for the feds. He knew Big Man was big on loyalty, but Big Man was never loyal to him. It was always to me and Derek. He knew how powerful I could get. That's why he tried to take me out how he did Pops. He was close, too. See, he was scared I would take the street shit from him when I never wanted it. I guess it was a misunderstanding that caused lives to be taken. This opened my eyes on how dirty these streets can be. Slam was Big Man's cousin from out of town, who he always wanted to be with Big Man. I never knew they were family until I was messing with his sister. He started coming around a lil' more when Big Man got locked up. He lived with a family member out of town. When he did finally come to town, he was under Big Man's brother's wing looking for love and guidance. Sometimes the wrong love or guidance can hurt you in the end. J knew how bad Slam wanted to be accepted and was willing to do anything. That same anything caused him to lose his life. The fact that he had the nerve to even have contact with his cousin's babymama let me know, nobody was safe. We thought it was another Slam because Big Man was told Slam moved around. They never said it was his cousin doing the dirt.

Slam was jealous and wanted to feel wanted. He never knew the loyalty I, Derek, and Big Man went by. He was taught something else and whatever it was, J taught him. When we were supposed to rob J's house, the plan didn't go as planned. The plan was to shoot us on sight. Because Derek took the gun from Slam, Slam couldn't shoot us like he was supposed to. It was two guns against one and me and Derek knew how to shoot very well. Slam didn't have a choice but to kill Derek. What he didn't know was Coby saw it. He also didn't know Coby watched, followed, and shot him. When Big Man's brother found out, he knew what time it was. He knew everything was coming to the light. He just didn't know how much time he had. He wasn't expecting me and Big Man to get in contact with each other no time soon.

When he found out, he knew it was crunch time. He had everything. He killed my pops and Derek's big brother, so why send Slam my way? Why tell me when I was younger you was gon' make sure the niggas felt the pain they put me through? It was him all along. Funny how life works. The same nigga that killed my pops, I was the one killing him. Laying in my bed, I don't feel no better. Killing doesn't make a difference. This was bigger than Derek. I wanted this my whole life, just for me to feel the same. I guess in a couple days, I'll feel better.

Wins And Losses
Chapter 13

A couple days went by and the police showed up at the house. Coby let them in, but they more so forced their way in. I didn't run or resist. I just smoked a cigarette and left with no problem. I told Endia to stop crying, that this is the life I lived, and to take care of my baby and Coby. She just stood there, crying her eyes out. I turned to Coby and told him to take care of the family, to stay in school, and to be better than me and Derek while he still got time.

"You keep yo mouth shut! I got this." I assured him.

"Not another brother." He cried.

The police threw me in the car and took me away. A week later, I appeared in front of the judge. I knew this was it. Right when I was done with this life, it came back around. I knew the fast life soon shattered. Just thought I had time to get out. By the looks of things, I waited too late and it shattered right in front of me. I never understood it, but I understood now. We get crazy days and even crazy nights. It's up to you to decide how you live your life or better yet, this life. I was born with a silver spoon, but I decided to take the wrong route. Even without a daddy, my mom made a way. Whatever I needed and wanted, I got. Guns excited me at a young age. Some things were out of my mom's control. Some things she didn't even know about. I followed in my dad's footsteps without even trying to. This life came naturally, even with us moving out the hood. Mentally and physically, I stayed in the hood. I had plans on doing the right thing, but sometimes things don't always go as planned. Now, I'm waiting to be sentenced. I just wish this didn't affect the people around me.

I've been sitting in this hell hole for almost two months, seeing my people through a small glass. I haven't even talked to my public defender. I'm lost in here. I just haven't folded. I seen a lot of niggas I know. A lot of us are fighting the same kind of case. My next court date makes three months. Hopefully I get some time instead of just sitting here continuously.

The first day they took me in, they had a million questions, but I had no answers. My fingerprints were on his door. Me getting shot helped them even more, so they say. The time and days were going slow. Luckily, my court date was here.

As I walked out, someone called my name. I knew the voice sounded and somehow felt familiar. It was Pop's voice, just how I remembered it. I'm probably tweakin', but I felt him hug me and heard him say, "I'm sorry this weight was put on you, son. I'm sorry I couldn't guide you and be here for you. I love you." I know it sounds crazy, but it was him. I don't know how or why. Sometimes the lifestyle chooses you like it chose my dad.

Epilogue

Thunder strikes.

"Mommy, you sleep? You crying? What's wrong?"

The thunder woke me up from what appeared to be a nightmare. A tear fell and my 3 years old was leaning over on me. My baby was his daddy all over again. The dream became a nightmare. The life his father lived is far from the life I want for my son.

Life can be a scary thing sometimes. Karma always comes back around and has the last say so. Even if you didn't do what was done to you, you did something. Losing someone makes it worse. We have to restore what the gutter took from us, and not let history repeat itself.

www.ingramcontent.com/pod-product-compliance
Lightning Source LLC
Chambersburg PA
CBHW020649250626
47154CB00008B/2882